Animals should definitely not wear clothing.

not wear clothing.

Written by Judi Barrett
and drawn by Ron Barrett

992126

Aladdin Paperbacks

For Amy and Valerie

Aladdin Paperbacks

An imprint of Simon & Schuster

Children's Publishing Division

1230 Avenue of the Americas

New York, NY 10020

Text copyright © 1970 by Judi Barrett

Drawings copyright 1970 © by Ron Barrett

First Aladdin Paperbacks edition, 1974

Second Aladdin paperbacks edition, 1989

Also available in a hardcover edition from Atheneum Books for Young Readers

Printed in the United States of America

10

Library of Congress Cataloging-in-Publication Data

Barrett, Judi.
Animals should definitely *not* wear clothing.

Summary: Pictures of animals wearing clothes show why this would be a ridiculous custom for them to adopt.
1. Animals—Juvenile humor. 2. American wit and humor, Pictorial.   3. Animals—Caricatures and cartoons. [1. Animals—Wit and humor]   I. Barrett, Ron, ill. II. Title.
[PN6231.A5B364   1988]   818'.5402   88-7825
ISBN 0-689-70807-6

Animals should definitely not wear clothing...

because
it would be
disastrous for
a porcupine,

because
a camel
might wear it
in the wrong
places,

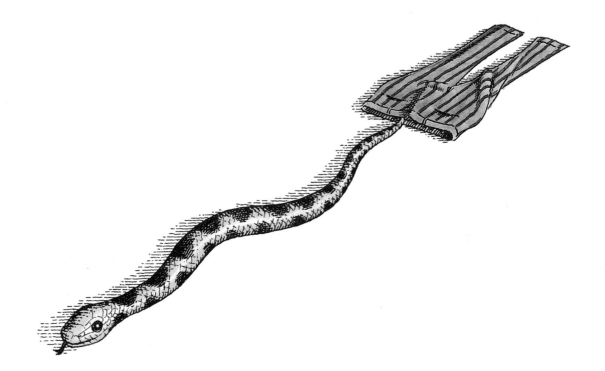

because
a snake would
lose it,

because
a mouse
could get lost
in it,

because
a sheep
might find it
terribly hot,

because
it could be
very messy
for a pig,

because
it might
make life hard
for a hen,

because
a kangaroo
would find it
quite
unnecessary,

because
a giraffe
might look
sort of silly,

because
a billy goat
would eat it
for lunch,

because
it would always
be wet
on a walrus,

because
a moose
could never
manage,

because
opossums
might wear it
upside down
by mistake,

and most of all, because it might be very embarrassing.